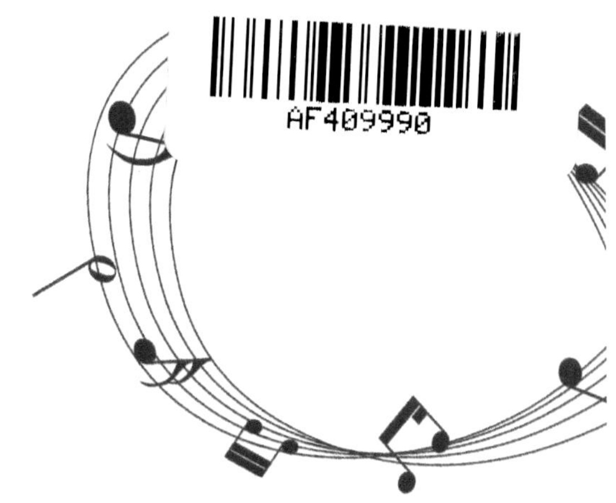

The Yellows

Tom Gammarino

Contents

For Leo, who sings like the devil

"And as long as people have problems, the blues can never die."

—**B. B. King,** *Off the Record: An Oral History of Popular Music*

The Yellows[1]

I'm sorry I'm not saying more," I said from the poolside lounger I'd been sunning myself on for the past week.

"Okay by me," said Claire. "Your only job right now is to rest."

"It's just that this day is so perfect. It's like it shuts off my mind entirely."

"That's good, honey. People study meditation for years before attaining such a state."

Baxter giggled. Claire was dipping the boy's little, pink feet into the cellophane waters of the shallow end.

I raised my shades and squinted. My doctor had instructed me to avoid direct sunlight for at least the first month, but on top of not liking to wear glasses in general, I hated the way they muted all those forms and colors out there. At the moment, I was fixated on the row of wildflowers along the fence. Who knew there were so many different purples in the world?

Just then, my uncle Len's docksiders came scuffling up the flagstone path. I straightened up and put my shades back on.

[1] Digital liner notes to Blind Seymour Wright's groundbreaking album *High as Hell*

flagstone path. I straightened up and put my shades back on.

"Seymour! How you enjoying your new equipment?"

We might as well get this out of the way ASAP: my name really is Seymour. I'd call it a coincidence, if I believed in them.

"There are no words," I said.

Of all the mental images I'd had to revise this past week, Uncle Len was easiest: tall, splay-footed and thin, business-casual. Today, he was wearing khakis and a loud, floral-patterned aloha shirt. His hair was gelled back, his transition lenses dark. It was no great mystery that I already knew what he looked like; unlike with my wife or son, who were far more beautiful than I'd ever have dared imagine, I'd *seen* Len before, almost every day of my life straight up to the accident.

"What are you doing here, Len?" Claire asked.

"I need to talk to Seymour for a minute."

"The doctor says he should take it easy for at least the first two weeks."

"It's okay," I assured her.

Claire frowned, scooped up Baxter, then went inside.

Len plopped himself on the chair beside me, elbows on knees. "These are nice chairs," he said. "What do you suppose something like this goes for?"

"I really have no idea. Claire's in charge of such things."

He nodded. "Look, Seymour, I wanted to come by and see if there's anything I can do to help speed along your recovery?"

"I think I'm good. My doctor says there's nothing like rest."

"Sure, sure. Well, your health is our main priority."

"I'm glad you agree," I said.

He studied the chair some more. I lowered my shades and studied the sky. For twelve years I'd been gazing at my *idea* of the sky, but what kind of sky is it that fits in a man's mind? The original was another thing altogether and permanently unhitched blueness from melancholy in my mind. Blue is joyous.

"So…have you picked up the old guit-box at all?" Len asked.

"How did I know that's what you were driving at?"

"I don't want to see us lose any ground, is all."

"Len, just give me one more day to relax, all right? I'll be back in the saddle tomorrow."

"That's what I like to hear."

"Good. Now go away."

"If not for me, then at least do it for your mother." He stood and tousled my hair the way he'd been doing since I was a kid. "Take it easy, Seymour. I'll drop by tomorrow." He scuffled up the path and disappeared.

I got up and went inside. Claire was breast-feeding Baxter on the sofa. They were watching some kids show on TV.

"What did he want?" she asked.

"Nothing. Listen, I think I'm gonna go up to the studio for a bit."

She crinkled her forehead at me. "You sure you're up to it?"

"Honestly, Claire, I feel better than I've ever felt in my life."

Which was, of course, the problem.

n my way up to the attic, I fetched a red, cinnamon-scented candle from the junk drawer. Christmas wasn't for another couple of months, but when I'd gone up to the studio the night before and flipped the switch, I'd found the light anathema to creativity. It was so *loud*. How could I compete with that? I'd tinkered for a few hours, but since I hadn't made any headway before descending, I'd thought it best not to mention it to Len. I hadn't had a new single out in the better part of a year, and he was going stir-crazy.

I sat in my usual chair, a swivel job I'd always imagined wrongly to be black (it was lily white). Taking up my acoustic, I strummed a few chords and waited for the gust of inspiration that would fly me from this austere room to that other realm where the songs grew, but my eyes were too preoccupied with these flickering walls and this wagging tongue of flame, this ubiquitous here and now.

I blew out the candle only to find I had a new problem. Rays of light streamed in through openings in and around the window fan. The room had gone zebroid. I tried closing my eyes, but how could I possibly keep them that way now I could see?

I sat there for an hour that afternoon, noodling and strumming, without ever once attaining escape velocity from the attic room.

went back outside. Claire and Baxter were sitting by the pool again. Baxter was scooping up water with a rubber spatula he'd filched from the kitchen. I picked him up. He giggled the most perfect little giggle you can imagine. I sniffed his head. It smelled of talcum powder, sweat, and, well, baby.

"Finished already?" Claire asked.

"I was finished before I started," I said.

"There'll be other days."

"I guess."

I flipped Baxter upside-down and held him by his feet. He laughed riotously, like there was nothing wrong with the world. Wasn't there?

"Mind if I take him for a walk?" I asked.

"You think you can handle it?"

"We won't go far."

"I should go with you."

"I'd like to brave it on my own, Claire, if you don't mind. It'll be a father-son bonding kind of thing. We'll just go up the street and back."

"And you'll call if you have any trouble?"

"Pinky swear."

"Then I'll get started on dinner."

I carried Baxter into the house, strapped him into his Bjorn, strapped the Bjorn on me, then went out the front door. It occurred to me this was probably the closest I'd ever get to knowing what being pregnant is like. As we bounced along, Baxter kept looking up at me, studying my face as if he saw something new there, as if he could see me seeing him. What made it even weirder was, while he clearly had his mother's head shape, he also very clearly had my own blue, slightly protuberant eyes.

Claire had once told me about some wacky early theories of

vision. Euclid, she said, believed the eye emitted light rays that struck objects out in the world, allowing you to see. It sounded ridiculous to me when I was blind, but now that I could see again, I empathized with old Euclid. Sometimes a person's gaze really does seem to affect your body. Baxter's, for instance, could be relied on to move the corners of my mouth up.

It wasn't long before we passed Len's house and arrived at the trailhead. Claire had taken me this way last week, two days after the surgery, while her mom watched Baxter. She'd wanted to show me the view from the ridge, which had been her main reason for choosing this house over the beach house in Santa Monica. I really hadn't been ready yet—someone transfixed by the sunsets of his own cuticles should *not* be shown a panorama that, in a single glance, takes in vast tracts of LA County and the Pacific beyond. I'd felt woozy and needed to sit down for a bit before we headed back. Claire couldn't stop apologizing.

Today, however, I knew I could handle it. No doubt Claire would disapprove, but it wasn't like it was much further to the ridge, a quarter mile at most, and I hadn't been kidding about that father-son stuff—it was important. My own father died in a coal mine outside Pittsburgh shortly after I was born. I had no memories of him and plenty of anxiety about how cut out I was for being a good dad, not having had a role model.

We left the pavement and embarked on the trail. Sure enough, the week of practice had heightened my depth perception, and I now had a much clearer sense of where my feet would land when I moved them. I also had less confusion about what was solid and what was shadow, though I still took extra care to keep Baxter's face far away from anything that might be a branch.

As we walked, I held a meaty baby thigh in each hand and alternately squeezed. Baxter was in stitches all the way to the summit. When we arrived, I took off the Bjorn and hoisted him onto my shoulders so his view might be that much better. It made me feel a little woozy again, but this time, I had a stronger sense of my own borders. To tell the truth, I almost resented those borders, since the cloudscape I'd been living in for twelve years hadn't had any, but I recognized that if I was going to live as a seeing person in the world, then it was worth knowing where my face ended and all that world out there began.

"What do you think, kiddo?" I asked, but Baxter didn't say anything. His mind was quiet. For the moment, we had this in common.

The next day, Claire made my favorite breakfast—oatmeal with bananas, pecans, and three types of berries that tasted like the colors they were. I bounced Baxter on my knee until Claire asked if I was expecting Len again today, at which point I put Baxter down and went upstairs.

This time, on my way up to the attic, I dropped by the bathroom, got out Claire's vaporizer, and filled it with water. In the attic, I set it on the desk before me and buried my head in the rising mist.

It worked well enough. My hands played notes. My ears listened to them. The sounds even took on colors the way they used to, but they were fainter than before. It was as if primary colors had faded to pastels and pastels washed out of the visible range altogether. In any case, there was nothing here to rival the galaxy of swirling cream in my coffee, the luster of Claire's hair, the warm pink cheeks of my baby boy.

"Seymour!" Len said, pretending to be a laid-back sort of guy. "I'm surprised to see you out here by the pool."

I knew he'd show up sooner or later. That particular twinge of anxiety had kept my thoughts spinning all afternoon.

"I tried," I said. "Nothing's coming. I haven't got any ideas. You can't force this sort of thing."

Len sat down beside me, same as the day before. "Damn it, Seymour. What seems to be the trouble?" The real Len was emerging.

I raised my shades, inhaled the technicolor world through my eyes, and lowered them again. "All right, Len. Here it is. I'm happy as hell, see. I'm happy like I'd never have believed possible. I mean, look at me. I've got a beautiful family, an amazing home, plenty of money, no health problems to speak of, and goddamn it, I can see!"

"I warned you, didn't I?"

"You were right, Len. It's like I've got the happy equivalent of post-traumatic stress disorder. Nothing gets me down."

"I know your little kingdom by the sea here seems perfect, Seymour, but trust me, there's plenty out there to feel blue about. There's war and climate change, famine, genocide. You've got oppression, repression, depression—"

"That's just it though, Len. For once I *don't* have depression. I don't have time to be diving inside like that. It's so nice out here in the world."

"Meh. Lots of people with perfectly good eyes take their lives every day. Look, Seymour, no one can blame you for enjoying your little spell of good fortune here, but sooner or later, you're gonna have to come down again. I'm not saying there's anything wrong with some happiness here and there. I'm not saying that at all. What I *am* saying is you'll die miserable if all you are is happy all the time. Trust me."

"Why should I?"

"Have I ever steered you wrong?"

"I don't know, Len. You certainly haven't steered yourself wrong, but Jesus, it's like you'd prefer to see me suffer."

"Come on now. I just want to see you live a meaningful life. I don't want you to have regrets. Think of your mother—"

"I wish you'd leave her out of this."

"She lives on in your music, Seymour."

"Get off my property."

"She wanted nothing more than—"

"Now!" I shouted, springing to my feet.

Len threw up his hands and beat his retreat. He made sure to get the final word in, though. "Go put it in your music."

Christ. I sat down and drummed my fingers on my abdomen. My thoughts were suddenly abuzz, and there was a real temptation to go pour it all into a song, though my greater desire at the moment was to flout my uncle's wishes. What I could not so easily flout, as I sat there swatting away nascent melodies, was this apparent obligation to think, and it wasn't just any sort of thinking I was doing, so much as exactly the sort Len had just jinxed me with.

I was thinking, in other words, of my poor mother, who'd never been able to forgive herself for my blindness. It wasn't her fault, though Coach McGeever *had* recommended several times that we invest in some contact lenses to avoid exactly the type of penetrating injury I eventually sustained. In any case, she certainly bore no responsibility for the right eye. That belonged to the overworked, overcaffeinated surgeon who made the still-impossible-to-fathom error of digging his scalpel into the wrong eye before a horrified intern stayed his hand. It made no sense for her to blame herself for this, though she pointed out, rightly enough, that were it not for the first blinding, there wouldn't have been the second.

In any case, the blame my mom took for my blindness was so complete she refused to file a malpractice suit and began going to church every morning after she dropped me off at the school for the blind. "How can you forgive me?" she would ask over and over, and I'd assure her I didn't blame her, but something kept her from moving on. She had finally managed, after all these years, to lift herself off my father's pyre, but this—this was too much. God would vanquish Satan once and for all in the end days, there could be no doubt about that, but for now the Evil One was racking up all these minor victories.

She'd give in to his seductions sometimes and commit the sin of pride by, for instance, crying herself to sleep. But this was no solution, since she had nightmares in which she'd be subjected to repeat visions of that fiendish orb homing in on my glasses and striking its target, yielding that awful, stomach-dropping *pwok*. She began doing the laundry way too often, like all day long, and she really seemed to be teetering on the brink of shit-flinging madness until, one fateful day, Uncle Len came by after school. He'd bought a guitar for me, and he played us a bunch of songs on the CD player he'd also bought. Songs by Blind Lemon Jefferson, Blind Willie McTell, Blind Willie Johnson, Blind Boy Fuller, Stevie Wonder and Ray Charles.

I wasn't wild about any of those songs, which sounded old-fashioned and sort of generic to my ears, but the point wasn't lost on me: *Here is something you can do with your life.* I picked up the guitar, and from that day forward, music gave purpose not only to my life but to Len's and my mother's as well. Especially Mom's. On hearing me play my first chord progression—a 12-bar blues in E—she rejoiced out of all proportion, and before I'd even written my first song, her singular focus in life became supporting Len in supporting me to become a career musician one day. And sure enough, after a decade of striving and the gradual, lonely evolution of a genre the critics would come to call "bluecore," I was making a pretty good living at this. The tragedy was, Mom died of cancer barely six weeks before one of my songs—"The Wrong I," the most literally autobiographical song I've ever written—spread like some seductive gene from a single college radio station (88.5, WXPN, University of Pennsylvania) to every musical brain in the land. Her most devout wish had come to pass, and she wasn't around to see it. It wasn't as if there'd been any ambiguity about what that wish had been either. Between doses of morphine in the hospice, she'd made me swear that no matter what, *no matter what*, I would continue to play the blues. Because music was a gift from God, and Satan might try to tempt me away from it one day. He'd put all kinds of stones in my passway, as the great bluesman Robert Johnson would have put it, and I had to be prepared.

"I won't stop, Mom," I said.

"Promise me!" she demanded.

I did what any mama's boy would do. "I promise."

Len smiled from the other side of the bed.

Mom pressed the button on the morphine drip. It was the last we spoke before she quit this vale of tears.

I lifted my shades and let the forms and colors crowd out my thoughts. Claire had bought a fluorescent, yellow foam thing for Baxter to float on in the pool. Currently it was folded over on itself on the stippled concrete, the sun lighting up the contours of its complex skin. It was beautiful, like everything.

It was only a matter of days before Len scuffled up the path again. He'd dropped all his other bands years ago back in Philly, so his financial prospects were always directly correlated with whatever I was up to, and for the however-many days it was since our spat, what I'd been up to was sunning myself on the lounger, walking with Baxter, making high-definition love to Claire, and generally enjoying my life. What I was not up to was making product.

Len sat in his chair. "I need to talk to you."

"Before you begin," I said, "I want you to observe the state I'm in. Have a good look. Notice how my muscles are relaxed, how I'm just lying here, supple and stress-free. Assume that I'm the same on the inside. Your being here may have raised my stress levels a little, but basically I'm still pretty relaxed. My heart rate is modest to slow, my spine is straight, my eyelids are relaxed. What's more, I keep saying 'relaxed,' which is itself a very relaxing word. Have you observed all this?"

"I have, Seymour. I have."

"Good. Now go ahead and start talking and watch how one word at a time you ruin my life."

"Actually, the reason I came here today was to say I'm sorry."

I waited for him to say whatever he was going to say next. It was taking a long time.

"There is no 'but'. I've been doing a lot of thinking this past week and I realized you're absolutely right. I'm a selfish prick. For years, I've been using you. I didn't recognize that's what I was doing, but I was doing it, nonetheless. I was selfish and manipulative, and I'm not going to subject you to that anymore."

"What are you saying, Len?"

"I'm saying I need to become more independent. That's what you taught me here the other day and I'm grateful to you for the lesson. What kind of selfish bastard would I be if I didn't celebrate your being able to see again? I'm happy for you, Seymour. It's so rare one encounters genuine happiness in this life. You have it and far be it from me to sabotage it for you."

"So you're saying what, Len? You don't need me to write any new songs?"

"I don't, Seymour. That's right. I don't need it. If you want to do it, great. I'll be happy to listen, promote them, whatever you want. But if you don't want to do it, well then you shouldn't do it. No one should force you to do it. This is your career. And more importantly, it's your *life.* Time for me to get better at understanding that."

"I see," I said.

"I know. It's great. So, here's what I'm going to do. First, I'm gonna sign up some new bands. I did it for years, I can do it again. Second, I'm gonna learn to play the guitar. All this time I've been counting on you to be my instrument, but it'll just be simpler all around if I get an instrument to be my instrument."

"I'll give you lessons," I said.

"I wouldn't ask it, Seymour. I won't ask anything musical of you ever again."

"Don't go overboard, Len."

"Think about it. Without me, you never would have become a musician in the first place."

"I might have."

"No, you wouldn't have. You know how I know? Because a true musician wants to play music all the time, regardless of what distractions might present themselves. What I realized about you the other day is you'd truly rather be doing other things. And you know what? That's fine! Go do those other things. Have a blast. For years I drummed into you this illusion that you were *meant* to play music, born for it, and blinded for it, and I really believed it too—it's important you understand that. But at the end of the day, *you* didn't believe it, and that makes all the difference."

"I love music," I protested.

"No, you don't. You've been brainwashed is all, and the sooner you realize it, the better it'll be for both of us. Here I am, Seymour, opening your cage. Fly away! Be free!"

The instant Len went away, I stormed inside.

"Everything okay?" Claire asked.

I didn't answer but went straight into the studio and picked up my guitar.

I strummed some chords and went looking for the music.

Couldn't find it.

I looked some more.

Still couldn't find it.

What if Len was right? What if music really *wasn't* my calling? Admittedly, I hadn't had much interest in it until my accident. I'm not sure I'd ever had the blues either. Once those forces entered my life, however, I was sure they'd be with me until I died.

And then I got the call.

"Blind Seymour Wright, do you or do you not wish to see?"

"I'm sorry?"

"I apologize for being so curt, Mr. Wright, but I thought it might keep you from hanging up. We've sent two letters care of your manager and had no reply."

"Who is this?"

"Mr. Wright, my name is Albert Findley. I'm with a company

called CXC Biotechnology. CXC as in 'see,' then 'not see,' then 'see' again. I'm calling because I want to invite you to be a part of a clinical trial involving a new cure for blindness."

"A cure?"

"For choroidal rupture blindness. The sort you have."

"Would you hold on a second, please?" I put the phone down on the counter. My heart was a speed bag someone was punching. I took a sip of my coffee, got punched some more, and picked up the phone. "May I ask what this surgery entails?"

"It's quite simple, really. We regenerate dead tissue using stem cells harvested from our patented metazoans and splice them onto existing tissue. The treatment has proven successful in clinical trials involving all four of the other great apes. We think it's time to add the fifth. Now, we chose you as a candidate because many of us here at the office are big fans, myself not least among them. *Philadelphi* was just visionary, if you'll excuse the pun."

The Oracle of Philadelphi was my second record, the one that had afforded us the move out west and our two houses on Olympus.

"Thank you."

"Thank *you*, Mr. Wright."

"I'll have to think about this."

"Of course you will. We anticipated as much. You can reach me any time at this number. In the meantime, you may want to have someone check out our webpage."

I didn't need to think much. I called back in an hour and set up the appointment. They could do it at the eye hospital downtown. When I told Claire, she was delighted. Len, on the other hand, tried talking me out of it. He told me to consider the professional ramifications, but I wasn't having it. I'd been waiting my whole adult life for this. My one worry was that if I made myself vulnerable to hope, and it all turned out to be bogus, I'd find myself in a very bad way. It never occurred to me that if the cure actually worked, I might find myself in a different sort of very bad way. But now here I was.

I looked some more for the music.

Still couldn't find it.

What I did find was a sort of epiphany. I don't know how it had eluded me until then. The long and short of it was this: happiness was preventing me from composing. If I wanted to compose again, I'd need, somehow or other, to get sad.

My first attempt was idiotic. I see that in retrospect. About five feet from my head was the attic door. It had a brass knob with a particularly menacing-looking lock mechanism on it. To be clear, I did not *want* to do what I was about to do, but that wasn't the point. I *had* to was all—for Mom, Humanity, God… And so, I pulled back my head as far as it would go to the left and slammed my right temple into the knob.

With an anticlimactic thud, icy-hot pain radiated outward from my temple and inward to my immortal soul. I wailed like I hadn't wailed in…ever. There were no words, just pure, unalloyed, a cappella pain. It was the most promising art I'd made in weeks.

As soon as the pain lost its edge, I wheeled my chair around, pulled my head back the other way and, again without thinking, bashed my left temple into the knob. I moaned and howled from the very sub-basement of my being. Words could not—and cannot—do justice to the pain.

The third round was something of a fiasco. I went straight on, forehead to knob, but my forehead must be pretty thick because the pain wasn't half as sharp. It didn't feel *good*, mind you, but it didn't quite cut into my essential animal the way I needed. I let out a little moan, but quickly curtailed it. You can't force this sort of thing.

I gave it one last shot. All I needed now to complete the circuit, to helmet me in pain, was an injury at the rear of my head. I got on my knees, facing away from the door, and touched my tender forehead to the floorboards. Then I flipped myself open like a butterfly knife and bashed the back of my head into the knob. This one hurt bad, hurt good. I caressed my head with both hands and watched the blood drip like melting candy down a white stripe of my zebroid room. The effect was dazzling, and I had several seconds to admire my work before blacking out.

"Seymour!"

I opened my eyes for a second, remembered where I was, and shut them again. The light was too loud.

"Jesus, Seymour," Claire said. "Are you okay?"

"What time is it?"

"It's nearly midnight. I came up to say good night. What *happened*?"

"Can I confide in you?"

"Of course."

I opened my eyes for real now. "In short, all this happiness is killing me. I can't write a song to save my life."

"Don't tell me you did this to yourself?" She stroked my head gently. It was sort of annoying. "Oh God, Seymour. How could you?"

"I used to be a pretty good artist."

"You were better than good."

"And now I can't write a single respectable verse."

"Maybe you need to take it easy for a while. It'll come back."

"A true musician wants to play music all the time."

"Where are you getting that? Len? It sounds like Len."

"Maybe."

"Oh, Seymour, you should know better than to listen to him. All he cares about is himself. You *know* that. There's no such thing as a true anything. There are only people. Forget about 'true.'"

This bothered me. She was such a nihilist sometimes. "One can strive for an ideal," I said.

"For Christ's sake, are you really complaining about being happy?"

"I'm a true musician," I said.

"Okay, you're a true musician. So what?"

"You just said I wasn't."

"Let's put it this way. Whatever you want to do, I support you. If you want to do music, great. If you don't, great. I just want you to be happy."

"You know what kind of music I write, Claire. Saying you want me to be happy is as good as saying you want my career to end."

"If you don't want to be happy, why did you sign up for surgery in the first place?"

"I've been asking myself just that. I *do* want to be happy, of course, but I thought I'd had enough despair to last me a lifetime. I thought I'd be able to draw on reserves, but actually it's more like out of sight, out of mind, or out of mind, out of sight, whichever it is. I was very bad at being blind. Some people, they're good at it, they don't mind so much. Your mom sounds like she was pretty good at it. Me, though, I always felt like I'd been cheated out of the world, and I got song after song out of it. But now I can see again, how can I be anything but optimistic?"

"Write an optimistic song then."

"How do you mean?"

"Write about all the things you're happy about. Forget the blues. Write—I don't know—the *yellows*."

Whether or not she had a soul, Claire could be pretty brilliant sometimes.

"That might actually work," I said, reaching for my guitar.

"Come to bed," she said. "You can invent the yellows tomorrow."

I surrendered, and we walked hand-in-hand to our bedroom, where she proceeded to dress my wounds and I proceeded to undress her. That she looked as good as she did still seemed like a sham—I had fallen in love with her for all the right reasons, after all. I kept wondering when the other shoe would drop.

Throughout my adolescence I'd held out hope for a miracle to cure my blindness, but by the end of high school I'd lost the lion's share of that hope and submitted to my mom's persistent wish that I get a guide dog to give me greater independence. Until then I'd sided with Len, who insisted I got along fine without having to take care of a dog to boot. But the idea that I was a bluesman who had yet to lose his virginity, let alone have his heart broken, weighed heavily on me, and lacking the enforced human contact that had come with school for so many years, I was unbearably lonely. My motivation for getting the dog, in other words, was clear: if I had a dog, I could go on dates, at least in theory. I had no idea, of course, that getting the dog would lead so directly into romance.

Part of the deal with obtaining a guide dog, see, was that the dog and I had to spend six weeks with a trainer, and Claire, as fate would have it, was our trainer. She was older than me, twenty-six at the time, but I had aged far more than a decade over the past decade, and for my part at least, it was love at first sight, so to speak. My dog was a German Shepherd named Mercedes. Day by day, Claire helped us get acquainted with one another, though from the first I was much more interested in acquainting myself with Claire. By way of small talk, I asked her why she'd chosen this line of work. She explained it was because of her mother, a moderately successful self-help writer who had herself been blind and depended on a guide dog to get around. Claire wasn't getting rich as a dog trainer, but she felt she was making a meaningful contribution to society. I admired this in her. I also admired her voice (spandex velvet and mango sorbet), and her smell too (one part English Breakfast, two parts spring rain). At her request,

I brought my guitar to one of our sessions and played her some of the songs that would eventually make their way onto my first album. One of them, "You Smell Right," I had obviously written about her.

"What do you think?" I asked while the last chord rang itself out. She was sitting very close to me now. I could feel her breath on my face, and sure enough, she smelled right.

"You're going to be famous," she said.

It was clear to me I had just arrived someplace I'd never been before. "Then you're going to be immortal," I said.

And then she kissed me. I swear for a moment I thought I was being kissed by the dog. Nothing against Claire's technique, but I had never been kissed before and had no hard evidence I was even kissable at all. As soon as I located Mercedes at my feet and knew for sure it was Claire who was kissing me, I abandoned myself and followed her lead. It was slightly disgusting and totally wonderful. I'd always worried that when the time came, I wouldn't know what to do, but there are some things the body just knows.

During a brief hiatus, I announced I thought we should have our next session at a restaurant.

"What about Mercedes?" she asked.

"I've been thinking a lot about that."

"Oh?"

"I don't know about you, Claire, but I believe things happen for a reason, and much as I enjoy Mercedes' company, she is very definitely not my reason for being here."

We kissed some more and then filled out some cancellation forms.

Our next session wasn't a session at all. Claire picked me up at home and took me to an Indian restaurant I'd never been to before. On Friday, she came to hear me play my weekly set at The Lamb Tavern; the following night we held hands while we saw/heard a play at Temple University; and the next Saturday, we took a day trip to the Jersey Shore. In short, I kept on ushering in my destiny, never once flinched, and within a couple of months—to my ongoing astonishment—Claire and I were engaged to be married.

To be honest, I didn't believe my mom when she told me how beautiful Claire was. I thought she was probably decent-looking, above average even, but when I got my first glimpse of her from my hospital bed after the bandages came off, I almost suspected malpractice again. I would have continued to love her no matter what she looked like, of course, but she looked like this! It was like winning the lottery twice. I'd heard about her auburn hair and hazel eyes, and my fingers had told me she was thin and symmetrical, but they had no way of conveying the whole radiant gestalt of her.

The next morning, I woke to the smell of fresh bread. Claire had been to the bakery. She greeted me with a bright smile in the bright kitchen, and I kissed her on the cheek. I dandled Baxter on my knee and admired the flowers on the windowsill while I wolfed down half a baguette with strawberry jam. As soon as I was done with my coffee, I thanked Claire and went up to the attic. For once, I decided to bring Baxter with me; the blues couldn't accommodate him, but the yellows surely could. He laughed and stretched his little hands toward the strings while I fingered some bright chords and improvised some lyrics:

Castle made of clouds in the dandelion breeze
Darling little creases at the backs of your knees
A jar of jam and a loaf of bread
A rhododendron and my rainbow head

That was pretty good! I wrote it down in my notebook, then composed some more. Claire came to get Baxter for his mid-morning snack, and I just kept on composing. I'd improvise something, write it down, then improvise something better and write that down. Darkness fell in a blink, and by the time I got hungry, I'd already filled half my notebook. I felt like I'd run a marathon and slain a dragon. I was so energized, I couldn't resist calling up Len to tell him the news.

"The what?"

"The yellows. As opposed to the blues."

"Cute."

"Are you busy now? I'd love to play you some of it. I think it may be the best work I've ever done. I feel like I was born again."

"Claire put you up to this?"

"You need to give her more credit, Len. She's a very intelligent woman."

"I'll be over in ten."

"Fantastic."

It was an hour before Len showed up—he could be a real dick

sometimes. Still, my enthusiasm hadn't waned. I was evolving a future. "I'm telling you, Len, I didn't think art could be deep and happy at the same time, but just wait 'til you hear."

"What the hell happened to your head?" he asked.

I ignored the question and launched right into "Rainbow Head."

> *Bright-eyed boy and my new guitar*
> *The good life used to seem so far*
> *The blues I knew and the red I bled*
> *Give way at last to this rainbow head*

As soon as I hit the last, exuberant chord, I looked up at Len. "Well?"

"Not to put too fine a point on it, Seymour, but it's fluff."

"Fluff?"

"Innocuous, superficial fluff. Be honest now. Would you really expect anyone to pay hard-earned money for that?"

"They might."

"They won't. People want depth. They expect it from you. This is all surface. I mean, what is it? It's an inventory. It's pretty enough, but it fails to *move* us. It puts our guts to sleep."

"Who's 'us'?"

"I've made a lifelong study of this. The average pop song goes deeper than that shit you just played for me."

"I think it's good."

"It's not."

"Get out of my house," I said.

"I'm telling you, Seymour, go do something else. Go play with your kid. Go eat some bread and jam. But God help us, spare the world this fluff."

Len had the good sense to leave before I broke my new guitar over his head.

I had always esteemed Len's opinion above all others, and this was no exception. Still, while his negative review of the yellows ought to have driven me insane, it did so only in a complex, tortuous way. After he left, I sat there for a minute assimilating, then descended to the bedroom where my unbelievably pretty wife was purring in her sleep. It wasn't long before the harder feelings departed, leaving in their wake only joy, that fluffiest feeling of all. I got into bed and tried to sleep, but I was so goddamned happy I decided to go downstairs and watch some TV. Maybe there'd be a depressing movie on or something. As it happened, there were several, and they were deeply cathartic; I felt purged.

Then the hand of destiny got involved again. I changed the channel and found myself watching a telethon for one St. Luke's, a hospital in Nashville that catered to kids with terminal illnesses. It wasn't but a few minutes before I found myself weeping, then taking out my phone and calling the number on the screen.

"Thank you for calling St. Luke's. Your donation will help save the lives of seriously ill children. How much would you like to donate today?"

"Oh, maybe two weeks."

"You'd like to volunteer?"

"Yes."

"Wonderful! Volunteers are the lifeblood of St. Luke's. What sort of volunteer would you like to be?"

"I'd like to give guitar lessons."

"Guitar lessons?"

"Is that unusual?"

"Somewhat, but then St. Luke's is an unusual place. May I ask who I'm speaking with?"

I told him.

"*The* Blind Seymour Wright?"

"You've heard of me?" I wasn't being facetious. I was quite well known among the musical set, though I hadn't ascended to household name status yet. He put me on hold.

"Mr. Wright?" a woman's voice said. "Is this really you?"

"It is."

"Mr. Wright, my name is Deborah Lingle. I head the business office here at St. Luke's. I also happen to be a *very* big fan of your music. Have I got it right that you'd like to volunteer some time with our kids?"

"That's right."

"Then let me be the first to welcome you aboard. We're honored, to say the least. Now, when would you like to do this?"

We hammered out the details.

I told Claire the news at breakfast the next morning.

"You're going where?" she said.

"St. Luke's."

"The hospital?"

"Yes."

"Why?"

"To get sad."

She put down the peach she was paring and shook her head. "What are you trying to prove?"

"I just have to do this. Music has been my life up to this point. I don't know how to live without music."

"But you're doing it brilliantly every day."

"*What* am I doing?"

"Living."

"It's meaningless."

"You're happy!"

"Some things are more important than happiness, Claire."

"Like what? Len's next Porsche?"

"Not that."

"Is this about your mother?"

How dare she ask me that?

"She was on morphine, Seymour. And you're being way too literal. She wanted you to be happy was all."

"Maybe it's just my ego, but I need to create something. If I can't do that, I might as well not live."

"What about Baxter?"

"What *about* Baxter?"

"You created him."

"I *re*created, Claire. You're doing all the real work."

"Look, I'm not against your giving sick kids music lessons. I think that's great. But do it because you want to make the world a better place, not because you want to get sad."

"Those strike me as compatible goals."

"But don't you see you'd be exploiting innocent kids?"

"I don't see it that way at all, actually. I would be suffering too. I would take some of it on."

"Seymour, these are *children.*"

"So? Isn't that all the more reason someone should give them a voice? Is it better all their suffering should go to waste?"

"There's something wrong about it."

"I'm an alchemist. I transmute suffering into gold. It's what I *do.*"

"You're planning to give them all the proceeds, then?"

"I might." I hadn't really thought about that. Money was beside the point.

She sighed. "Why don't you just gouge your eyes out if being able to see makes you so insufferably happy?"

"Believe me, I've considered it." I had, too. "Thing is, it wouldn't be the same if I *chose* it."

"Well, aren't you choosing *this*? What's the difference?"

The question frustrated me, the insolence of it.

"It's different," I said.

She sighed and resumed paring her peach.

The staff at St. Luke's welcomed me with oodles of southern charm and a dinner reception in the grand ballroom. Mostly I ended up hanging out with Deborah Lingle, who turned out to be a fellow martini drinker and an honest-to-goodness fan, one of the most ardent I've ever met. I'd call it a wonderful coincidence, if I believed in them.

"Your albums got me through menopause," she told me. "I kid you not. When I heard you wanted to volunteer for us, I was flabbergasted. A prophet in our midst!"

It's always nice to hear how my work has affected someone, but it can get a little weird too. There's just something profoundly disconcerting about the idea that my fan base might be made up of *individuals.* It's difficult to explain.

Anyway, the hospital's president was a very large man named Reed. On the dais before dinner, he sketched out my own recent medical journey, which he'd read about in *Scientific American,* and pointed out how cell-level cures in any field of medicine were a great inspiration for them here at St. Luke's. The audience, consisting mainly of terminally ill children and their prematurely aging parents, applauded with a fervor and regularity wholly incommensurate with anything I might have deserved. It was almost enough to make me think my plan could work, because clap by undeserved clap, I was beginning to feel sad.

I slept intermittently in my Spartan guest room, ate griddle cakes in the cafeteria in the morning, then made my way to the atrium where Reed had recommended I give my lessons. It was a good room, classroom-sized, but wood-paneled and warm, with oriental rugs and a large window overlooking some centuries-old oak trees and a white gazebo. I was glad to see the guitars I'd donated were lined up in their cases against the wall. I took one out and set it on a stand, then arranged a couple of chairs to face one another. To my surprise, I was feeling nervous. I'd never given a guitar lesson before.

At 9:00 a.m. sharp, Reed ushered in my first student. I consulted the roster he'd given me. "This must be Sarah?"

"That's right," Reed said.

"I'm very pleased to meet you, Sarah," I said.

Sarah smiled, tight-lipped and shy. She was small and pitifully skinny, with pale blue eyes and skim-milk skin. She wore a baseball cap, as so many of them did.

Reed had told me all about Sarah over dessert the prior evening. He'd told me about all my students, but I remembered Sarah best because she was just six years old. She'd been diagnosed after her grandmother discovered a lump along her spine when she was three. A conservative estimate had her dead in two months. I hated myself more by the second. That was progress.

Reed left us to our lesson.

"What sort of music do you like?" I asked, not at all sure how appropriate a question this was for a six-year-old.

"The Beatles," Sarah said.

I was impressed. "What do you say we make a deal that you'll be playing a Beatles song before I leave this place?" I extended a hand to shake.

She smiled that same tight-lipped smile again and shook the hand.

"Do you have a favorite song?" I asked her.

"'Let It Be,'" she said.

This choked me up for some reason, and instead of talking, I turned Sarah's attention to the Baby Taylor acoustic on the stand beside her and gestured for her to pick it up. At three-quarter scale, it was still a bit big for her, but not so big that we wouldn't be able to get anything done.

"Is this…mine?" she asked in an incredulous little voice.

"As much as anything is ever anyone's, Sarah, this is now officially your guitar."

She beamed.

I began by teaching her how to sit properly, how to cradle the guitar and grip the pick. I taught her about frets and got her to memorize the open strings. Her first homework assignment was simply to spend ten minutes looking at the guitar, just looking at it. I myself had never had the luxury as a fledgling guitarist, but I remember wishing I could see what I was doing in those early days, and I wasn't going to let my years of blindness make a sensory chauvinist of me.

Over the next two weeks, I gave five private lessons each to thirteen kids ranging in age from six to fourteen. I taught them music with all the attention and love I'd have given my own son, and I was amazed by their strength and determination. They'd drag themselves in after chemo or who-knows-what indignity, looking elderly with exhaustion, yet still, somehow, every bit the energetic, life-loving kids they were.

Evenings and weekends, I drank martinis with Deborah Lingle, swam in the pool, and read from the Bible in my nightstand. I kept meaning to get out and see a bit of Nashville, country music capital of the world, but I found I didn't really want to leave the hospital. I had so little time, and some of these kids might have even less. Things happen for a reason, I kept reminding myself, though for the life of me I couldn't fathom what that reason might be.

Before our time together was up, Sarah had learned to play a halting, three-string rendition not only of "Let It Be" but of "Hey Jude" as well. All thirteen students learned to play some song or other, and the concert we put on the night before my departure moved me to smiles and tears at once. Reed had asked me before the show if I'd be willing to end with a set of my own, but I told him that this evening belonged to the kids, not me. I wouldn't have had the right songs anyway. Instead, I just sat back with a palpably disappointed Deborah Linglo, drank some iced tea, and listened to my students play the songs they'd worked so hard on to a packed house. Those kids were beautiful up there, every one of them. When we reached the end of the program, they got the standing ovation they deserved.

Then, to my surprise, Reed introduced the encore they'd secretly prepared for me as a going-away tribute:

Amazing grace, how sweet the sound
That saved a wretch like me.
I once was lost, but now am found,
Was blind but now I see.

I was overwhelmed with sadness, which ought to have been a good thing, but what I'd failed to take into account was the manifold quality of sadness, its many *types*. My songs had grown out of the sadness of loss and regret whereas this new sadness was foremost the sadness of pity—and pity is not an altogether heroic feeling. In effect, pity says *There but for the grace of God go I*, which is really another way of saying *I'm one lucky motherfucker*, which, as far as sentiments go, is about as far away from the blues as one can conceive.

So, while my time at St. Luke's had failed to induce the sort of feeling that might compel me to write songs, it was by no means without practical consequence. A couple of days before leaving, I dropped by Reed's office for a little heart-to-heart, then walked to the bank down the block to transfer some funds. It seemed the least I could do for these kids. As a bonus, it was bound to make me some other kind of sad.

Claire picked me up at LAX in the Mercedes. The top was down, and Baxter was giggling from his seat in the back, his thickening hair blown all over the place. I patted his head and planted a kiss on my wife's cheek. My family was still far more beautiful than I could believe.

"How was it?" Claire asked, pulling away from the curb.

"Where to begin?"

"Before you do," she said, "the weirdest thing. The pool cleaner called to tell me the check I wrote for him this morning bounced."

"Oh."

"That's it?" Claire said. "That's all you're going to say?"

"Do you want to hear about my time at St. Luke's before I tell you where the money went? So you'll have some context?"

"Jesus, what did you do?"

"Imagine Baxter is dying of some terrible illness."

"How much did you give them?"

"And there's a procedure that might fix him, but we can't afford it."

"How *much*, Seymour?" She was growing fierce.

"All of it," I said, feeling giddy.

Claire's face went pale, and she pulled over on the side of the road. "All of *what*, Seymour?"

"All of our *money*, Claire, what do you think? Checking, savings, IRA. All of it."

She sat up straight, swallowed something invisible and huge. "You have to get it back."

"I can't."

"Of course you can. They'll understand."

"I don't want it back, see, is the thing."

"You *will* want it back when you realize what you've done. Tell them you went temporarily insane. It's not even a lie. Get *some* of it. Get half."

"They need it more than we do. Do you know how much a bone marrow transplant costs?"

"People don't *do* this, Seymour! What did we work so hard for all those years? Jesus, what's happening to you?" She buried her head in her hands and sobbed. Baxter seemed to find this hilarious. I regretted twisting Claire's guts up like this, but I also knew this sacrifice was for the greater good, and not just the good of sick kids or even the good of my art, but good in itself, good for the good of Good.

"I don't even know what to say. I have no words for you right now."

"People study meditation for years before attaining such a state," I said.

That did it. Claire commenced beating the shit out of me with her fists. It hurt a little, which was neat. When she was all punched out and sobbing, she got out of the car, took off her heels, ran barefoot down Century Boulevard, and disappeared around a corner. I bided my time in the car, new songs queuing up in my brain. Claire had left Baxter in his seat, so I was pretty sure she'd be back. Anyway, I couldn't have driven off if I'd wanted to—she had the keys.

She returned some thirty or forty minutes later, though not at all in the manner I'd expected. She'd put her heels back on and fixed her hair, and the way she walked oozed self-confidence. When she got close enough to the car that I could see her eyes, I was taken aback by a whole new weather system in them: the storm had passed.

She got in the car and started the engine. "Do you think I'm stupid?"

"What kind of question is that?"

"Did you think I wouldn't see what you're trying to do here?"

"Save dying children?"

"Come on, Seymour. The jig's up. You want me to pack my bags and walk out on you, right? So you can be miserable and get back to writing music? So you can be a 'true' musician? A true bluesman? Well, guess what, Seymour, *fuck* you and your little designs, okay? Because I am not going to give you the satisfaction. No way. From now on, I'm going to devote myself to making every second of your life sheer bliss. We'll sell off your guitars and this car maybe, and, trust me, I will find ways to make our new middle-class existence feel like the choicest sort of luxury. Oh, you're in for it now. If you think the last few weeks have been good, just you wait and see. You will want for nothing, absolutely nothing."

She proceeded to mix up a bottle of formula for Baxter, to unzip my fly, and to suck the words right out of my head.

As soon as we got home, she put Baxter down for a nap and led me hand-in-hand to the attic, where she had already unwittingly instituted phase two by renovating my studio. She'd bought new furniture, all maple and feng shui; the walls were decked out with photos of rock gardens and streams, and there were plants greening each corner of the room. Worst of all, she'd installed a skylight, and the room was now canopied in bright cerulean. One could compose the yellows here perhaps, but never the blues.

The rest of this period—I haven't the slightest notion how long it lasted—passed in a kind of stupor. I was vaguely aware of roasted lamb, fresh fruit, bubble baths, martinis, music, some very distinctive brownies, a plumpening Baxter bouncing on my knee, Nutella, blowjobs galore, and copious amounts of sleep. The overriding sensation was of a very capable hand gently massaging the underside of my brain.

It was only in the dark of our bed, on one of those however-many nights, that language began clanging through my skull again like the tongue of a tolling bell.

I'd slept like the proverbial baby until the non-proverbial baby in the adjoining room began crying at 2:43 a.m. in the most grating frequencies available. Claire rushed to slake Baxter's desires, but the boy was in rare form tonight, and before she could restore the peace, I'd sat up, appraised my situation, and determined to do something about it, something desperate and last-ditch. I knew I couldn't afford to waste a second. I closed my eyes, listened to Baxter's colicky wail, and heard in it the distillation of all animal suffering, the spilled blood and snapped bones, the whole carnivorous pageant. It wasn't long before I'd harvested my terrible idea. It was perfect, the sacrifice required of me so absolutely counter-instinctual and blood-curdlingly wrong that I could never really want it as much as I *didn't* want it. There was nothing I wanted less, in fact—except a meaningless life.

Claire would be back any second, and she could not be allowed to lobotomize me again. I reached into her nightstand and found the little box of thumbtacks we used for hanging calendars and things. Taking out a dozen, I stuck them one-by-one through the elastic band of my boxer shorts, wincing as they pierced the flesh around my waist. I thought of stars, thorns, burrs, of Saint Francis of Assisi and Joan of

Arc. It didn't matter what I thought of, so long as I thought. Eventually, Baxter shut up, and Claire slipped back into bed with me. I feigned snoring. Throughout the night, whenever the drowsiness began to overtake me, I'd agitate the tacks, target some new nerves, and jumpstart my thinking. The temptation to nap was overwhelming, but I fought it to the last and didn't let myself get any more sleep. I did, however, let Baxter get his.

As soon as my firstborn, onlyborn son let out his first cry of the morning, I made sure I was there, cribside, waiting. I cupped my hand over his tiny mouth, kissed the soft, baby-smelling head, and carried him softly through the kitchen and out the back door, pausing only to pocket the multi-purpose peeler from the junk drawer—even then, I couldn't countenance a knife. Things might have turned out very different had I not also knocked the cheese grater off the counter on our way out. The racket it made would have woken the dead, and to this day I have to wonder to what degree this was or wasn't an accident.

"Seymour?" Claire called from the bedroom.

I cupped my hand even tighter over Baxter's mouth and tiptoed along the flagstones.

"Seymour?"

We set off running. I knew we'd have a considerable head start: Claire slept nude in the summer and would have to put on her robe before emerging from the bedroom.

Sure enough, we were clear past Len's house when she called out from our front lawn, "Seymour! Where are you going?"

I stopped and turned. "Oh hi, Claire. I'm just taking Baxter for a little walk. It's a father-son kind of thing. You can go back to bed." I knew she wasn't going back to bed. I'm not even sure I wanted her to.

"Seymour, do you know anything about the blood on our sheets?"

Jesus! The whole neighborhood would hear. As I fumbled for a suitable reply, she began walking toward us on bare feet. I had a decision to make. I thought about calling the whole thing off, playing innocent, and trying this again some other day, but I knew that if I blew this, I might never get another chance.

So I ran. In no time, I reached the trailhead and raced up the hill, bounding over roots and stumps and ducking under jutting branches to protect my boy's eyes, as if that made any sense. As soon as we got to the ridge, I laid Baxter out on a large gray boulder, stripped off his diaper, and held the peeler over his snow-white abdomen. He giggled. He thought I was playing some sort of game. There were all sorts of games I'd hoped to play with him one day, catch chief among them. Board games too. Monopoly, Scrabble, Trivial Pursuit. And cards. Go Fish first, then one day Blackjack and Poker. Maybe we'd go to a casino together on his twenty-first birthday, win a bunch of money at the roulette table and go pay it back to the strippers. It was only when my little fantasy reached this point that I knew it for what it was—a temptation—and cast it out with the devil.

Claire gained the ridge. As soon as she laid eyes on us, she gasped and grabbed hold of a vine to stabilize herself.

"Keep your distance, Claire."

"Oh God! Seymour, this is madness!"

"Just to be clear, I don't want to do what I'm about to do."

"Then *don't do it!*"

"I have to do it. That's the point." *No matter what*, my mother had said. That was our pact.

"Jesus, Seymour. What good can come of this?"

"*Meaning*, Claire. I'm not a nihilist like you. I want my life to amount to something. I'm obeying a higher calling. You wouldn't know anything about it."

She struggled to catch her breath. So did I.

"Be rational for a minute," she pled. "There must be another way. I'll do whatever you want. Forget all I said the other day. I was upset. We'll work something out. Just don't hurt Baxter, *please*."

"If you do what I want, I'll be happy."

"Then we'll do the opposite of what you want. How about that?"

I thought about this for a moment and gave my sincerest reply: "I want Baxter to live a long, happy life. I want that desperately."

It was the truth, and it was more meaning than Claire could bear. Her eyes rolled up in her head, and her body toppled to the dirt like one of those car dealership balloons when the wind dies down.

Gently, I began scoring Baxter's viscera with the serrated edge of the peeler. I didn't assert enough pressure to break the skin, but it was more than enough to convert his ticklish laughter into frightened crying. It was also enough to make a stream of apple-juice urine arc across Los Angeles and saturate my sleeve, which was most unpleasant. I took hold of Baxter's little pee-pee—thoroughfare for the grandchildren I would never have—and pointed it away from me until the urine trickled to a stop.

I *had* vaguely wanted grandchildren. I regretted that my mom had never gotten to meet Baxter. She would have spoiled the pants off him. As a kid, I'd always enjoyed visiting my own grandparents. Freedom has its privileges, of course, but to grow old without children always seemed to me such a lonely destiny. How much better to have a house full of descendants to keep the darkness at bay.

Mark it: temptation number two. The thing about faith is you can't sneak around the side of it. Thinking will never get you there. At the end of the day, you either have it or you don't. I had it.

The time was nigh. I held the peeler a couple of feet above my quaking son and took one last look around. Claire was still lying there, useless, on the path. I could sacrifice the boy now without the least resistance, just as I'd designed in bed. Within a matter of minutes, I could be inconsolably miserable, but something stayed my hand. Without quite knowing why, I put down the peeler, took out my phone, and called up Len.

"Hey there, Seymour. What can I do you for?"

"I'm at the ridge. Claire's passed out on the ground, and I'm seconds from sacrificing my son."

"I see," Len said—he didn't seem especially surprised by this turn of events. "Don't do anything irreversible. I'll be right there."

I took up the peeler again and sat beside Baxter on the boulder. He'd stopped crying. We just sat there for a bit, father and son, enjoying each other's company. I apologized for what I was about to do to him, assured him I had no desire to do it but that the divine Will had published the commandment in my brain, and everything happens for a reason. I told him how I'd hoped he would get to do all the things in his life my blindness had barred me from doing. I told him he would always be special to me and that I loved him.

And there it was: temptation number three. I kissed my boy's forehead one last time, then hardened my heart. I had cleared my passway of stones.

It couldn't have been two minutes before Len showed up in pinstripe pajamas.

"Keep your distance," I said, resuming my former position over the boy. I pressed the peeler into his abdomen. He resumed crying. It was a kind of music.

"Seymour," Len said. "What the hell do you think you're doing?"

"I'm a real musician. It's my destiny to be miserable."

"Then your reasoning is impeccable. This will definitely do the trick. It'll also land you on death row."

The prospect of jail and such hadn't entered my mind until now, but it was hardly a deal-breaker. They'd let me play guitar, wouldn't they? Even if they didn't, I was pretty sure I could filch some utensils from the cafeteria and rig up some kind of instrument.

"Look, Seymour. In a way, this whole thing is my fault. I want you to know I recognize that. Your whole life I've been training you to think in terms of performances. Even now you're performing. Why else would you have invited me here? You needed someone to watch. But look, Seymour, this is not a performance, okay? This is *life*. Look around you for a minute. There are no eyes here but ours. No one is watching you but me and poor Baxter there. Your mother is dead and gone. Whatever promises you made to her live in your head now and nowhere else. The sun is not an eye. And posterity, Seymour, it's an illusion, a cruel one at that—it doesn't even exist. All those ghosts in your head aren't real. I swear to you they're not. They're just stories you're telling yourself. It's just us here, and you can bet there's no God of Abraham who will stay your hand at the last moment. If you kill the boy, you will have killed the boy, neither more nor less."

I looked down at the glinting peeler in my right hand, and then at the wailing boy whose soft chicken body heaved under me. His legs were levitating several inches above the rock, his face crimson, tears pouring steadily down his cheeks from terror-stricken blue eyes that were my eyes but new, eyes that were emitting rays that were affecting my brain, tunneling beneath my deepest convictions, uprooting my very sense of who and what I was.

The peeler stabbed into the dirt at my feet.

"That a boy," Len said, lunging in and seizing Baxter. "Everything's going to be okay now."

"You don't have to *lunge*," I said.

Len gave me a consolation smile. My mother's younger brother was proud of me. And he was right, of course: everything *was* going to be okay. As soon as I owned up to this temporary psychotic break and spent a few weeks in some institution or other, things would return to "normal." We might even get some of our money back. Yes sir, I was going to be happy, and happy-go-lucky, with my gorgeous wife and my growing son, my mansion with its brand-new skylight, my gleaming Pacific, and seeing all of it, every second of every blissful day for many long, vivid years…

I picked up the peeler—

"No!" Len cried.

He was too late. I'd thrust the blade straight into my right eye. There was a white-hot fire in my brain, exquisite agony, poetic pain.

"You idiot!" Len said.

I wiped off the blade on my pants, then lifted it to my other eye and took in the world of particulars one last time. I was sweating profusely, and my heart was pounding in my chest, but I was determined not to make a big deal out of this. The world was very beautiful, and I was glad to have seen it again. That was all.

"You know what?" Len said. "Go ahead and do what you have to do. Nothing I can say will stop you."

And now I was the one made proud: Len finally understood about destiny.

I looked over at Claire, still passed out there on the ground. The greater part of me, I confess, wanted to wait until she could wake up and bear witness to my heroism, but while I disagreed with most of what Len had been preaching a minute ago, he was clearly right about one thing: this was not a performance.

I'd played my heart out to any number of empty bars back in the early days. The human soul is the only stage that matters. I used to know that.

Hot jelly spattered onto my hand.

I hope you enjoy the record.

"TOM GAMMARINO writes novels of deadpan surreal fantasy—imagine Philip K. Dick having a drink with Kurt Vonnegut in the *Star Wars* Cantina" (*Honolulu Magazine*).

He is author of the novels *King of the Worlds* and *Big in Japan*, and the novella *Jellyfish Dreams*. His short stories and essays have appeared in *Interzone*, *American Short Fiction*, *The Writer*, *The New York Review of Science Fiction*, and *Tahoma Literary Review*, among others, and he eo-edited *Snaring New Suns: Speculative Work From Hawai'i and Beyond* (Bamboo Ridge Press). He holds an MFA in Creative Writing from The New School and a PhD in English from the University of Hawai'i, and has received a Fulbright fellowship in creative writing and the Elliot Cades Award for Literature, Hawai'i's highest literary honor.

Bibliography:

BIG IN JAPAN, Chin Music Press, 2009

JELLYFISH DREAMS, Amazon Kindle Single, 2012

KING OF THE WORLDS, Chin Music Press, 2016

Connect:

Website: tomgammarino.com

Twitter: @gammarino

Facebook: facebook.com/tom.gammarino

BLACK HARE PRESS is a small, independent publisher based in Melbourne, Australia. Founded in 2018, our aim has always been to champion emerging authors from all around the globe and offer opportunities for them to participate in speculative fiction and horror short story anthologies.

Connect: linktr.ee/blackharepress

A Great and Shifting Sea

by John Leahy

The traveler had explored almost every corner of Monsiel and had enjoyed the experience, but he absolutely hated wet-soil environments. Swamps, marshes, bogs…curse them all. His appetite for knowledge of the world's various creatures and plants had pushed him all over the continent. He'd climbed to the top of treacherous, icy mountains and had dived to the beds of rivers and bays. Dangerous ventures all, but none as sapping, and spirit-draining, as wading through miles of rushes, muck, and water-pools. Pools which were sometimes quite deceiving. What often looked like maybe a few inches of water could turn out to be a foot and a half deep. A foolishly trusting step into one of these beasts and one ended up moving forward in misery after water had flooded over the top of one's boot and down inside.

He looked at the boy walking a little ahead of him. Of course, the boy never blundered into a deep pool. He seemed to have an almost supernatural sense regarding them and only stood in ones that were actually as shallow as they appeared.

"It's not much further now," the boy said.

He'd met the boy in a tiny village on the patch of land between the Toliad mountains and the bog itself. He'd been passing through the village when a gaggle of children, poorly attired barefoot urchins, had gathered around him, walking beside him as he made his way onward. To get rid of them, he threw some coins to his left and right and sped up his progress as they scattered to retrieve the money. He was almost clear of the village when he saw an older boy up ahead, standing outside a hut. The boy was watching him intently as he approached and fell in step with him as he walked by.

"You're a soldier," the boy said.

"Amongst other things," the traveler responded.

"What other things might these be?"

The traveler had looked down at the boy upon hearing this. Usually when boys saw a sword at a man's side, it was the only thing about that man they remained interested in. He'd decided to humor the boy.

"I study things. Nature. The world around us. Animals and plants, mainly."

"I can show you a very special plant. A tree. A tree the likes of which you've never seen."

"I've been all over this continent, boy. I've seen every type of tree it has to offer."

"Have you ever been to the heart of the Yexan bog?"

"No."

"Then you haven't seen this tree. And there's four of them. In a little grove."

They were clear of the village now and the traveler stopped walking. He looked the boy in the eye, testing his mettle. The boy returned his gaze, unflinching. There was intelligence there, and strength. Not your average, timid village child.

"Describe this tree."

"Black. Leafless branches. Strange, gold-colored flowers sprouting from some of the branches." The boy paused. "Over a hundred feet high. Thorns over a foot long."

The traveler remained silent as he tried to see such a tree in his mind. It sounded like a drunkard's dream.

"The thorns are alive," the boy continued.

"What do you mean?" the traveler asked, his brow furrowing in irritation. Was this boy perhaps some sort of mentally unwell fantasist? A foolish poetic dreamer of a sort?

"I've seen them killing fairies."

"Killing *fairies*?"

"Yes. By stabbing them and sucking their blood."

"Really."

"Yes. I swear it. I'll take you to the grove for ten gold coins."

The traveler snorted. "Ten gold coins?"

The boy's eyes dropped to the traveler's sidearm. "That's not the sword of a poor man."

The traveler smiled humorlessly.

"How far is this grove from here?"

"About a day and a half's walk. If we leave now, we'd be there tomorrow evening."

Part of the traveler was frustrated that he was even entertaining this story, while another part was intrigued by it. He knew a little about small carnivorous plants that inhabited bogs. Due to the poor nutritional content of the soil in bogs, some of the plants that grew in them derived their food from insects, which they trapped and digested. These he found interesting enough, but a carnivorous *tree*! And one that got its sustenance from *fairies*!

"I'll give you five coins now, and five when I see these trees in front of me."

"Alright." The boy extended his palm.

The traveler deposited coins in the boy's hand. As soon as the fifth coin jangled against the others, the boy's hand closed and disappeared inside his pocket.

The traveler cocked his head back in the direction of the village. "Get yourself some bedding and some food. Meet me back here."